THE MIDNIGHT SCRAWLS

FATEMA POCKETWALA

Virgin Leaf Books

ISBN 978-93-88942-91-1

First published in India 2020 by Virgin Leaf Books
An imprint of Leadstart Publishing Pvt Ltd

Sales Office:
Unit No.25/26, Building No.A/1,
Near Wadala RTO,
Wadala (East), Mumbai – 400037 India
Phone: +91 22 24046887
Email: info@leadstartcorp.com
www.leadstartcorp.com

Disclaimer: The Views expressed in this book are those of the Author and do not pertain to be held by the Publisher.

Editor: Tanzeel Saiyed
Cover: Darshana Dhakan
Layouts: Ashwini Jadhav

About the Author

Fatema Pocketwala worked in an Advertising Agency for a few years before she decided to start an Art Décor business for herself. She loves travelling and reading, both preferably together.

Acknowledgements

A special shout out to my dearest parents who never stopped me from being the wild child of the family and always encouraging me to follow my dreams to my heart's content.

The Midnight Scrawls

Fatema Pocketwala

He did not have a smartphone to keep checking

his children's pictures on social media

But he had a picture in his wallet which captured

their innocent souls

High above the clusters of clouds,

Looked just like candy land

The earth below,

Became a tiny painting

Problems which gave her sleepless nights,

Became distant memories

The never-ending sky,

Made her imagination run wild.

The shades of blue vibrant and many,

No colour pallet could replicate

*Her naked body
was a sight to devour,
But the demon himself
was afraid of her soul.*

He gave her white roses,

Next year, it was a bundle of yellow rose

Each year after that, he gave her

red roses,

Which lay on her grave to wither.

Fatema Pocketwala

Her eyes proved she spent sleepless nights.

His ashtray was never empty.

Love lost, Ego won.

She feared leaving her parents

The thought of living with someone

else scared her

Her freedom would be curtailed

Her life would seem different

The thoughts kept playing in her mind

Till the day she met him for a purpose

called arranged marriage.

Small innocent faces became the heart-breaking
stories of the Syrian War.

Posts were shared,

They even tweeted about it,

The world spoke and spoke about the cruelty,

But the innocent faces yet continue to become
the sad stories.

The world talked about humanity, but forgot to
implement it.

Fatema Pocketwala

Battles were fought,

Bullets were fired,

Houses became ashes,

Religion became war.

Amidst all this they all thought

they were clouds of thunder.

But no one knew someone

sitting high above was crying,

Over how mankind destroyed

his perfect creation.

Her smile was again infectious,

The tear ducts dried up long back.

The brain had full control over the love-struck heart.

But a small part of the heart had cheated slyly,

With the hope that he will come back to her.

As the depression settled in,

The parents gave up on him,

The friend's circle started decreasing,

Colleagues called him a psychopath.

While the others around just drifted away,

The only one who stayed back and lent

his shoulder to cry on,

Was the four-legged creature who never left his side.

Fatema Pocketwala

They both sailed in the same boat,
Of doubts,
Self-pity,
Uncertainty,
Criticism,
Lost love,
Depression,
Anxiety...

But they rowed the boat together to a
shore where only love existed.
The right company made the world
of a difference.

People will hurt you. Maybe not just once.

You may get betrayed a thousand times over.

People will use you for your kindness and leave you

with a broken heart.

But let your heart be the brave one.

The stronger one. The wise one. The kind one.

Don't become them.

You keep loving and caring the way you do.

Let your heart not lose its compassion.

Because that is something no one can take away from

you.

She heard the song again and again,

They thought it was her favourite one.

But no one knew that every word of that song,

reminded her of a life full of memories.

Family disowned her

Society taunted her

Friends disappeared

A lesson learnt

A broken shoe and all alone in the

big wide world.

She thought it was the end.

But years later, she was to remember it was the

beginning of her walk to fame.

Fatema Pocketwala

"I have so many things on my bucket list, that I
want to do before I turn 25," she said with a
spark in her eyes.

"But I have only one thing on my list, till the end
of time," he said looking at the sky.

"What's that," she asked.

"To spend the rest of my life with you,"
he said with a confident smile.

Fatema Pocketwala

Even if there is no night,
I'd still be your guiding light

Even if there is no air,
I'd still breathe you in your scent everyday

Even if there are no stars,
I'd still be your shooting star

Even if there is no caste,
I'd still follow you like religion

Even if there is no color,
I'd still love your shade

Even if there is no war,
I'd still fight a battle for you

Even if there is no poverty,
I'd still beg for your love

Even if there is no sand,
I'd still build a castle for you

The stage witnessed her marvel every day
The pole and drapes were her props to use.

Her dance so pure,
Felt like an offering to God himself.

Her moves so sensuous,
Just like the stars seducing the night.

Her flips so smooth,
As natural as the water flowing.

Her eyes so expressive,
Making each feeling shout out loud.

Her passion for dance so evident,
Would make anyone wonder if she was
the creator of it.

It was a stormy day,
But thunders were a wonder
The sunlight was harsh,
But warm on her skin
The weather was biting cold,
But she loved playing with snow
She finally started seeing good
in the bad too.

Fatema Pocketwala

She was bound behind the walls of limitations
She glimpsed freedom through the tiny holes
of those walls
The glimpses showed her a new scenario
every time,
A scenario she wished to live,
Those glimpses were enough for her to break the
walls fighting against all odds.

He dominated her dreams every day,

But his face was always a blur.

The day their eyes met in a crowded room,

She knew he would stand beside her till

the end of time.

"Time heals everything,"
they kept telling her.

Little did they know, time was something
she just did not have.

A heart broken

A tear shed

Depression settled in

The anti-depressants became a habit

But the brain yet withstood all this.

They met years later on a crowded street,

This time not as strangers,

But as long-lost lovers.

She penned down poems in his love

And stories of his betrayal.

But a day came,

When she fell short of words and letters.

The writer in her finally helped her to get over

him.

He wanted a well-educated girl

A girl he could show off proudly

Someone who could stand out in a crowd.

But the day she opposed him,

The male chauvinist in him woke up.

They knew her to be the bold one

They wanted her to be the strong one

They expected her to keep smiling.

She did oblige everyone.

But her tears didn't stop because she

wanted her own special someone.

She was a backpacker,

He a doctor.

He brought the stability and she brought the

youth back in each other's lives.

She realised, years later,

That maybe he had to enter her life,

If only to teach her a lesson.

Not to trust someone wholeheartedly

That looks can be deceptive

That trusting someone is easy

But when that trust breaks

It breaks a part of you.

At the mention of his name

Her pulse yet quickened

Her lips always trembled

Her hands would shake

Memories would come alive

And a tear never failed to escape.

But that was just it,

Because the last time she saw him,

He looked lovingly in the eyes

of another girl.

Fatema Pocketwala

Their conversations started after
they wished each other goodnight.

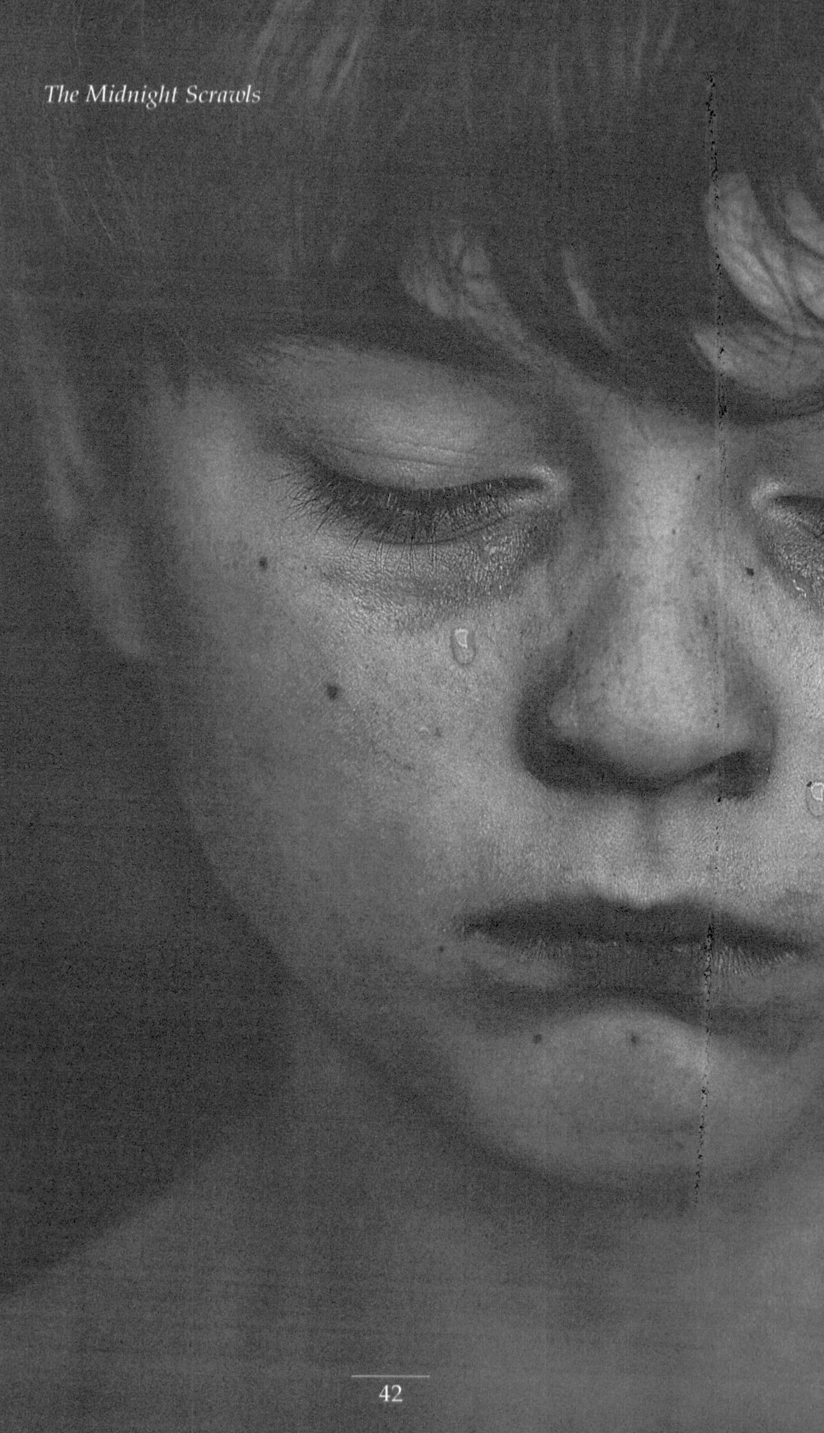

Fatema Pocketwala

While some kids died of a chemical attack,
The bodies of others yet lay unmoving below the rubble.

Some just disappeared like thin air,
While some others are guests for just another few hours.

The world saw and read about the cruelty,
It even brought tears to everyone's eyes.
But the world, it seemed, had turned its heart to stone.

Defeated is what she felt every time a no came,
But she kept hope in a small place in her heart
but a part of her heart felt defeated,
She wanted to shout and ask God a question,
I am not bad, I must have made many big
mistakes, but I am not bad. I have a kind heart.
Then why with me every time.

You will sometimes feel that you can't breathe. You will want to give up. The feeling is going to be horrible. Your heart will just want to forgive him, let go of all his short comings, you will just want him to be your present and future. You will need all of him. You will want to let go of your ego a thousand times over to have him stand beside you, holding your hand and whisper sweet nothings.

So, don't let go ofsomeone you love. It's not worth it. Worth it is when you fight to make that love survive, giving it a second chance.

In a world full of people ready to give up on love, be the one who fights till the end to see it bloom.

Fatema Pocketwala

Sometimes,
make a random decision.
Take a risk.
Push yourself beyond your limits.
Loose control.
Drive on a bumpy road.
Just to see what lies ahead.

At the stroke of midnight,
People wished one another a happy new year
Some made new year resolutions.
Some got a little happy high
Many partied the night away
Dancing, crackers, lights, long drives
The city didn't sleep the whole night.
While on the border,
The night so quiet,
Where the sound of their wishes echoed,
The only wish being to meet their families
again safe and sound.

Wagging their tails,
Wide eyed, all the bundles looked at her with joy.
She picked the one which lay alone,
All by itself in one corner.
"Why did you have to adopt that?"
Her mother asked.
She looked down at the kitten which was black
from head to toe,
"To break stereotypes," she answered.

They met during their chemotherapy sessions,

Each with a story to inspire the other.

Years later, they walked out of the same

hospital with their little bundle of joy.

Fatema Pocketwala

The teacher turned the page to the last

of the book

Explaining why war was an evil doing

The bomb was dropped on the school

While everyone lay there unmoving

The pages of the book swayed in the wind

amidst the rubble.

Theirs was a love-hate relationship,

He left small insects in her wardrobe to scare her

She spoke up for him even when he was wrong

He hid her clips and always lost them

She stayed up late to watch him work

He stood as a shield for her

against every passing storm

Her shoulder always popped out

when his head was about to fall

A tear in her eye would make his heart melt...

The story went on for years to come...

They described this bond as the brother sister duo!

Her fat and curves were a little too obvious

Her diet regime lasted a week to be precise

Green tea seemed like poison to her

And junk food was the love of her life

Exercise was a task in itself.

But she looked back on those days and

laughed out loud

Because all that now seemed was a part

of her being

But not out of necessity any more.

Somewhere between wanting to become a

doctor to the late nights in the hospitals.

She wished to relive her teens again.

Fatema Pocketwala

As the music started playing

The girl bound to the wheelchair felt a quiver in her legs

Within minutes she was dancing to the tunes

Her parents finally realised her passion for

dancing did its own small miracle.

Strained relationships

A little bit of more ego

A concept of " I, Me, Myself"

Non - acceptance of rejection

Actions on the rebound

A thirst to live all alone

Everything played against him.

He blamed it on karma,

But little did he know this was just a

bad chapter of life, not meant to last a lifetime.

As she lost the competition to her rival,
There wasn't a trace of sadness on her
vibrant face.
The mother rejoiced with tears in her eyes
as she lost to her daughter.

.

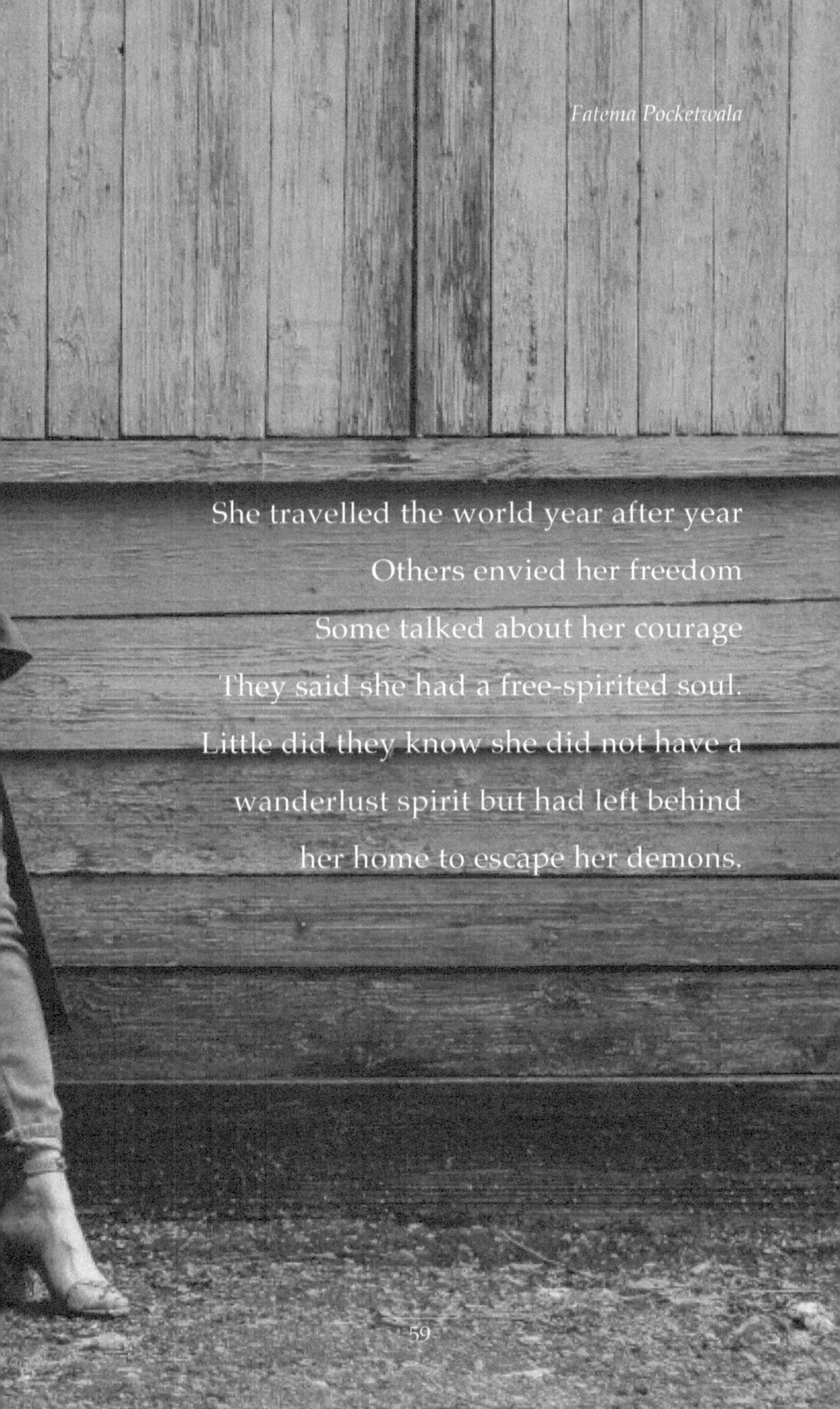
Fatema Pocketwala

She travelled the world year after year

Others envied her freedom

Some talked about her courage

They said she had a free-spirited soul.

Little did they know she did not have a

wanderlust spirit but had left behind

her home to escape her demons.

His traits were that of a playboy,

Known to work hard but party harder.

But the day he brought a girl to meet

his mom,

His mom knew he was finally growing up.

Beer bottles kept getting empty,
The waiter kept on refilling the glass with
scotch on the rocks,
The night went on,
But there wasn't a moment of silence...
The father and son were finally having a heart to
heart conversation.

Both were unaware of the love they shared

Friends, family, strangers,

Even the camera lens saw the love.

Realization came when it was time to

walk away.

"My scars run deeper than skin.

I can never heal them," she whispered.

"Then let's try healing them together," he said

She didn't believe in fairy tales.

But then one fine day a helicopter ride, a ring,

a few red roses and three words changed it all.

"I want to lick all of it," she said wickedly,

"You can't do that," he said in a daze.

After a lot of persuasion, he finally

became her partner in crime.

The five-year-olds were caught red-handed

licking the cream off the cake.

The journey of their love story,

Was one with many hurdles.

Tears were shed when alone,

Tears were shed when together.

Both were sure of the love they shared,

But the world never believed.

They met secretly,

Just to see the sparkle of love in each other's eyes.

The world doubted their love a thousand times,

But they proved them wrong each time.

They proved to everyone around,

That true love can withstand distance, fights,

society, tears and a lot more.

This wasn't the end of their battle for love

It was the start of their happy beginning.

Loving parents.

Perfect job.

Doting boyfriend.

High spirited friends.

Happening parties.

But her most dazzling smile

appeared when she inhaled the

smell of old pages of novels.

You have been going through hell,

And I know that well.

But as they say,

The sun always shines after a rainy day.

That sun will shine for sure,

If not sooner than later.

Things will fall into place,

And you won't even know.

And one fine day,

When you open your curtains,

The morning rays will touch your face,

And you will know that things are falling into place.

*You will discover what an amazing and awesome person
you are,*

And the child in you will come alive once again.

You will find that someone special,

Who will allow you to be the child all over again

And he will have your back,

Every tiny step of the way.

Dear Universe,

To whoever who rules it. To whoever decides how it operates. Thanks for letting me see the sunrise day after day, thanks for letting me live another day. Thanks for all that happiness, care, love, hope and faith you give me every day. Thanks for the loving souls in my life. Thanks for taking away the bad which passed by me, without me noticing. Thanks for all the things you give me every day, which I take for granted. Thanks for the strength to make it to another day, when all I have wanted was to give up. Thanks in advance for all the good you will get my way, for all my wishes which you will grant day after day.

Sorry for all the times I was a bad being. For maybe at some point in life being the reason someone cried themselves to sleep. Sorry for all the mistakes and all the bad thoughts.

So, make me wiser, don't let me ever stop being the kind soul that I am. Don't let any bad take my good away. Keep all those bad thoughts away. Grant all my wishes, make them come true, give me my own miracle to believe in. You know what's in my heart, you can read and feel it much clearly than me. Give me my own MIRACLE to believe in.

Love,

A girl eagerly waiting for her miracle

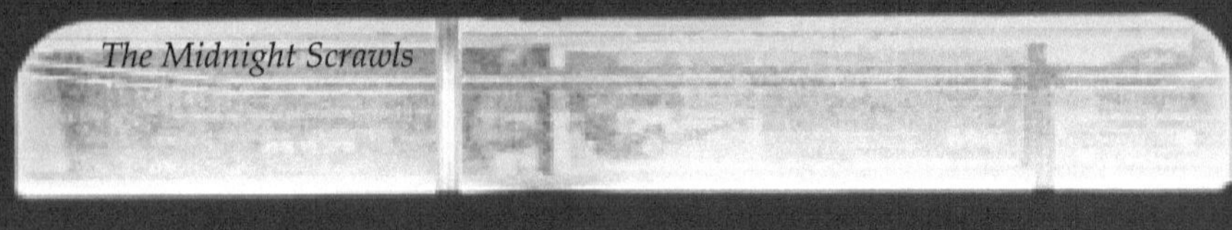

"Stop making them fight. They have been best friends forever", said the Heart.

"And they say that humans are the smartest creatures", laughed Misunderstanding.

He thought his smile was normal,

But it brought a blush to her face every time.

He thought himself to be the normal guy next door.

Little did he know,

Just one smile and a tight hug could make her blush more than a bride.

In a world where everyone moves on
Be the person to cry it out
Show emotions
Cherish memories
Continue traditions
Be the warm hearted one
Lower your pace
Admire the sunset
Take a pause to help someone
Be thankful...

Because at some point in life you will look back
and either have happy memories or you will
regret not having any.

Fatema Pocketwala

You will meet a sweet girl,
And you can then call her yours.
She will complete you in ways,
For a lifetime long.
Your smile will be a blush,
Every time someone mentions her name.
Your morning greetings,
Will be full of love and care.
Your goodnight greetings,
Will hold a promise to hear her voice
the next day.
Your eyes will search the crowd eagerly,
Just to see her smiling face and
her smile so bright.
Your thoughts of ME,
Will become thoughts of US.
Your heart will care a bit more about her,
Than about you.
Each time you falter,
You will have her hand to hold on to.
Your stressful days,
Will become bearable with her voice so sweet.
You will have something in life to look forward to
Maybe a peck on the cheek.

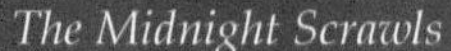

We may be divided by continents

We are discriminated on the basis of colour

We follow different religions

We pray to different gods

We learn from different holy books

But it's basic

We all are humans

And that's what's important.

"What a pro you are at lying,"
her friends always told her.
But neither could her eyes
Nor the quiver of her lips
Or her actions could lie
When she told him she did not love him.

They met at a place where Jesus and Moses rest,

Where the land is holy and the sea is at rest,

Skeptical as they were to talk to each other,

Unknown from the fact they were meant

to be together,

Forever and ever.

I still feel the pain

I still have tears at the thought of his name

I still have hope in my heart deep inside

I show the world that smile

But I am dying a slow death inside

I don't know if he's right or wrong.

Who am I to judge

When it could just be Karma telling me, you are

just paying for what you did long back.

He always made her feel in need,

But the day the right one came along,

She always felt needed.

The difference made her realise what true love is.

Fatema Pocketwala

They both met for a couple
dance for their friends sangeet.
A year later, heir bodies moved in
perfect sync on the dance
floor to celebrate their wedding.

He leaned in close to her and whispered

in her ears, "Will you be mine?"

"Forever and ever," she said with a smile.

They made their own little promise

during the Pheras.

Fatema Pocketwala

The trip faced many hurdles even before starting,

But it turned out not to be a random trip,

Just a bag full of memories.

Everyone wrote a chapter in each other's lives.

Which upon reading will bring a smile till eternity.

It wasn't just a road trip

It was a treat for their eyes

The mountains danced all around them

The river's flow made the sweetest noise.

The only smoke was the burning wood

The air so fresh it made them nostalgic

The trees so dense it made them wonder

The roads so curvy it made them faint

The stars so bright it guided them through the

night.

Sometimes it's hard to stay positive
You keep getting hurt again and again
Attempts at anything keep failing
Failure becomes your shadow
Rejection becomes a habit
But how helpless you feel when
you can't do anything
Because what's meant to be will be.

She hid her tears,

Behind her dazzling smile.

The scars were hidden,

Beneath those magical cosmetics.

But she only raised her voice in protest,

When history repeated itself.

This time with her daughter.

Fatema Pocketwala

How do I keep hope on a rainy day when
there is no sun or moon to show me the way,
she said out loud.

In response, the thunder struck and the
whole world lit up.

They talked and talked,

Discovering a new thing about each other

every day.

They laughed together making head turns

at the sound.

They teased one another on their past lives.

The deep dark secrets were shared when the

night was quiet,

And each one felt the pain for the other.

The good night messages,

Made each sleep with a contented smile.

While the morning greetings,

Made their whole day pass in a dreamy state.

But months later as they passed each other

on the crowded street,

Each bent their head to avoid the contact

of eyes,

Trying to act ignorant, of what they shared.

Somewhere at that time, life laughed at

the irony.

Prep talks

Complaints

Soul searching

Talks of a bright future

And after venting out all the suppressed feelings later...

The tears this time were finally happy ones,

As she finally let him out of her heart.

The brain finally sighed with relief.

She penned down poem after poem

About the love she had for him

Memories they made

His smile and his soothing voice

Future dreams she weaved with him

And also his betrayal.

The pen whispered to her, "I want to

pen down your happily ever after now."

But the heart whispered, "Not Yet."

She walked the stage
To the sound of heavy applause
The happiness lighting her face up
The proud faces of her parents
making her smile wider
The journey of 3 years
The struggle, the pain, the tears,
The uncertainties, the long nights,
the early mornings,
Making her feel prouder,
That day she rose higher in her eyes.
And it all became worth it
When she held the trophy for the second
time.

The Midnight Scrawls

Both were like two pillars

Helping her stand tall

When all she wanted was to fall down

Holding her high

When she wanted to bend low

Supporting her sides

When the ground kept shaking

They said they were her true friends,

While for her they were her two guardian
angels,

Flapping their wings to save her from every
passing storm.

92

While she hated every aspect of her job,
The only thing which kept her sane
during office was the chocolate boy whom
she kept aimlessly staring at.

Her brain kept finding reasons to stop

loving him.

Her heart rejected all reasoning.

But the day a stranger gave his all just

to get her to smile again.

Her heart was finally freed from all his memories.

94

The night seduced him with dreams of her

each day.

While the harsh rays of the sun each morning,

made him face reality again.

Fatema Pocketwala

As he let go of her hands

Leaving her standing alone with no one to turn to

Not even a glance in her direction again when

she shouted out

Walking away leaving her alone to face the storm

The scenario in her dream woke her shouting

Dreams made her realise what reality could not.

The light of dawn outlined the mountains

A sight she would behold to keep her sane

The early morning chirp of the birds sounded

better than her playlist

The slow motion of dawn to sunlight was like

a magical picture

But her heart yet skipped a beat only when he

wished her a morning like always.

She let the sunlight in again
Dark rooms no longer existed
A flicker of a smile crossed her face more often
The tears had finally dried up
Sounds again became music
Facing the world no longer a task
She finally was winning her battle against
depression.

And one fine day she decided to say bye

Just like that

Without a care or a thought

She did what her heart told her

And ignored her brain royally

Some thought it was her rashness

While others did not care

While some just thought would someone else

ever laugh like her

Or call out their names like she did

But then they yet needed to test their friendship,

Would it withstand time, or the distance

Each wishing in their hearts for this to not be the end

but just the beginning.

Fatema Pocketwala

People say you will meet someone better

Someone who will make you whole

Whom you can trust blindly

Someone you will make lifelong memories with

The brain gets that

The heart is where the problem lies

But what to do it has always been a slow learner.

As the brain shut

the box full of memories.

The heart yet had a secret key to them.

Fatema Pocketwala

They said memories will fade

The hurt will not last forever

The heart will heal

The brain will see reason

The soul will connect with another

But at that moment all she had

was memories to live with.

As the storm broke out,

She sat huddled in her car that had fallen in a ditch,

He came like a saviour,

Her knight in shining armour,

Not all storms are bad,

She thought when he carried her away.

She finally overcame her fear of storms that day.

Fatema Pocketwala

She walked towards the stage to receive her

law degree

Her family cheered her

Their eyes held pride in her as she continued the

family tradition

While the dancer in her wished to take

the stage for another reason.

The tears did not stop each night

Her thoughts took her places where nothing existed

Her lips quivered every time she took his name

Her cries in the night begged for help

She fell a little faint every time she saw his face

She knew she was in a place worse than hell.

Sometimes people will tell you to

have faith.

Not lose hope. Keep going. Believe. Trust.

But sometimes you need your

own miracle to trust in.

While he always got up early,

He would never leave the bedside,

Waiting silently to see her rise

from slumber and smile.

Sometimes you will have to be

an optimist,

If only to console your heart.

They heard the music,

And knew the groom arrived,

They expected the groom to appear dancing

amongst his friends,

But what they saw,

Was the bride dancing her heart away

While the groom followed her as she led the way,

While some were shocked,

The others knew the bride loved

breaking stereotypes.

Fatema Pocketwala

A house in each land
was how rich he was,
They often asked him
where his home was,
The day the priest pronounced
them Man & Wife,
He knew home would be where she was.

The Midnight Scrawls

Fatema Pocketwala

The chaos
Fights
Madness
Rush
Tears

Were all worth it in the end when they both said,
"I Do".

Calm and patience was what he kept,

While he taught his dad how to drive the car.

The father wiped the tears rolling down his cheek,

As he remembered that he never had the time to

teach his son to even walk.

He scored goal after goal

And led his team to a victorious score

But his shout was the loudest

And his jump the highest

When the kid called him dad in broken

words for the first time

That's what he called a goal.

She promised him she would love him

till her last breath

While he held her hand in a tight grip,

"Promise me you will move on and let me

be only a memory," she said to him as she

breathed her last on the hospital bed.

The young nurse standing silently behind realised

that it's not words but intentions and actions that

prove that love really exists.

While she deleted all her chats with him,
The screenshots yet filled up her album.

Her paintings cost people their fortunes
A glimpse of her canvas left people speechless
She grew from an amateur to a world
renowned artist at the speed of light.
But her mom yet treasured the paintings which
she drew when she was just a kid,
That's when she was the proudest.

Street smart businessman

Tough nut to crack

Heart of steel

Jet set lifestyle

Cunning brain

Biddings and takeovers

All these adjectives seemed futile when

he took his just born in his hands.

The Midnight Scrawls

Fatema Pocketwala

As the war broke out in his land

The houses crumbled

The cries for help became louder

The bodies lying around grew in numbers

The sound of bombs and bullets became unbearable...

That's when he feared life, not death.

The child kept humming the tune repeatedly,

They thought it was his favourite tune,

Little did they know the melody and the crime

scene kept haunting him.

Love hurts. It's not always about the happy days. There are days when you want to walk away. When you don't want to fight for it. You reach a limit. The hard days will come.

If not sooner, later.

The love only survives if you are ready to look beyond the unbearable days and fight for the person you may hate for the moment.

Her wild and carefree imagination,

Led her to write some world-acclaimed scripts.

Little did people know her imagination took her

places where her demons lived.

It was her blessing and curse at the same time.

They called her a night owl,

But she thought herself to be a night traveller,

She relived memories,

Made plans for the future,

Analysed every word of a sad song,

Made up situations,

Wrote poems hearing the silence,

Stared into darkness,

Discovered a new talent,

And waited up to see the slow motion,

From dawn to sunrise.

All this just to feed her imagination.

While the world moved on,

Sending symbols on Whatsapp to express their love.

He wrote a letter the traditional

way to keep the flame alive.

Unknown that he would be her future-to-be.

They went on dates every now and then

And made memories which are yet fresh.

But then it was time for him to go away to

a far-away land,

Each cried thinking how would they survive

But each was strong for the love they shared.

Memories were relived.

No stretch of land or ocean could lessen the

love they felt.

Their own love story too had their share of

ups and downs.

But both were sure of thing, the love which they felt

within their hearts.

And now she stands tall with him, sure of a future

brighter than the sun.

For now, they are Mr & Mrs.

The time old proverb seemed to be haunting them,

That not all friends are meant to stay.

She never had hatred in the heart,

But it seems she lived in a hateful heart.

She was a dog lover,

He loved cats.

Both fought over which

one to get home.

A few months later, both

got their bundle of joy to look after.

They promised to spend their lives

together;

They lay in their graves next to each other,

Forever and ever.

Fatema Pocketwala

His heart skipped a beat

When he saw her walk

down the aisle

He kissed her cheeks.

Someone in the crowd

captured the happiness on

the son's face when he gave

his mom away.

She loved the drama.

He loved cricket.

The fight for the remote

was a daily affair.

That's when their romantic

night usually started.

Everyone talks about love

But they forget to tell you about

The misery

The pain

The uncertainty

The doubts

The fights

The hatred

The tears

The journey whose end may

not always be love.

You are stronger than many people I know
You hold your head high even when
you want to bend it low
Those tears in your eyes are not that hard to drop
You have walked on many difficult roads which have
just increased your strength
You may wish to cry right now
But you are worth more precious
than you are lead to believe
Life goes on, they keep preaching you
But then you got to do just that even if you don't
believe in it
But I do believe one thing,
That you are going to get up again and that smile
will again be whole
Your laugh won't be fake
And your tears won't be sad anymore
Because you are a fighter and that's the way you
are born.

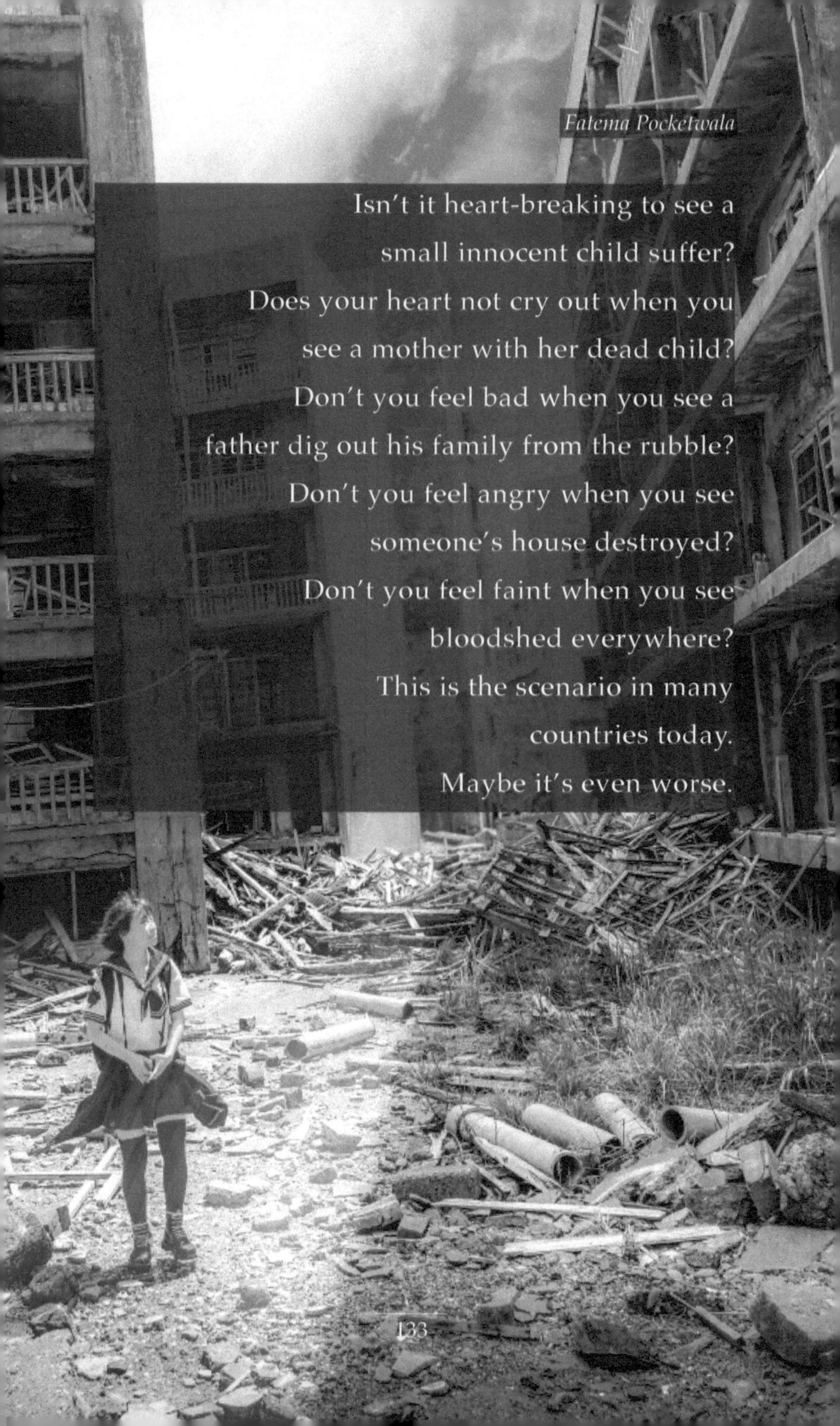

Fatema Pocketwala

Isn't it heart-breaking to see a
small innocent child suffer?
Does your heart not cry out when you
see a mother with her dead child?
Don't you feel bad when you see a
father dig out his family from the rubble?
Don't you feel angry when you see
someone's house destroyed?
Don't you feel faint when you see
bloodshed everywhere?
This is the scenario in many
countries today.
Maybe it's even worse.

Dancing

Clubbing

Night outs

Partying

This was freedom for her.

Until she went to a place where

the thousand twinkling stars

made up for the disco lights.

The perfect groom

Big fat wedding

Lovely dresses

12 carat solitaire

Attentive bridesmaids

Lavish decorations

Sparkling jewels

All became a blur

And her heart skipped a beat,

When she saw her first love walking up to her.

You behaved a little naughty,

So, this was the result.

But what a beautiful result.

When you hold it in your arms

It will be your own small miracle.

When you hear it cry for the first time,

It will be the sweetest sound.

It's first smile will be more precious

Than watching a thousand shooting stars.

Its body so tiny

You will want to protect it more than you.

Hugging it to yourself for the first time

Will be a memory which you will remember till eternity.

Maybe it's not a miracle...

But maybe God's own gift for you.

Her tantrums, she tolerated

Her ill-behaviour, she defended

Her insults, she smiled away

Her late nights, she kept awake

Her depression, she stood like her pillar

Her fears, she soothed

Her enemies, she faced

Her wrongs, she corrected

Her sadness, brought tears to her eyes

Her happiness, her prayers

The step-mother, loved her with all her heart.

While she only saw her as a thorn in her life.

She realised the love she had for her years later,

When that's exactly what she did for her

own daughter.

How do you tell someone that everything in life hurts. That breathing is a task in itself. The heartbreaks, the betrayals, the hatred, the pain, everything has broken you down.

The only thought that gives peace is of eternal sleep.

How do you tell someone that you are falling. In a dark hole. That your heart does not have the courage to climb up that hole because you know there is no hope.

How do you tell someone that you cry yourself to sleep every single night. And that no dreams can haunt you, because the thoughts of a bleak future terrified her.

But be the one to tell people that you kept fighting.

That something in life kept you going, and you did see the light after a long time.

That no matter how hard life can get, the bad times never lasts forever.

The sun always shines again on you, if not sooner then later.

Tell people that we all have a warrior in ourselves, who's strength to fight those hard times is much more than we think.

He lived across the street from her place,

She stood in her balcony every night to

watch him staring out.

She went for a jog to see him every morning,

She overcame her fear of dogs to play

with his poodle.

Little did she know, he made the same efforts to

get a glimpse of her.